David A. Adler

Mama Played Baseball

Illustrated by
Chris O'Leary

HARCOURT, INC.

Orlando   Austin   New York   San Diego   London

Requests for permission to make copies of any part of the work
should be submitted online at www.harcourt.com/contact or
mailed to the following address: Permissions Department,
Houghton Mifflin Harcourt Publishing Company,
6277 Sea Harbor Drive, Orlando, Florida 32887-6777.

www.HarcourtBooks.com

Library of Congress Cataloging-in-Publication Data
Adler, David A.
Mama played baseball/David Adler; illustrated by Chris O'Leary.
p.   cm.
Summary: Young Amy helps her mother to get a job as a player in the
All-American Girls Professional Baseball League while Amy's father is
serving in the army during World War II.
1. United States—History—1933–1945—Juvenile fiction.   [1. United
States—History—1933–1945—Fiction.   2. All-American Girls
Professional Baseball League—Fiction.   3. Baseball—Fiction.
4. Family life—Fiction.]   I. O'Leary, Chris, ill.   II. Title.
PZ7.A2615Mam   2003
[Fic]—dc21   2001006865
ISBN 978-0-15-202196-2

E G I J H F

Manufactured in China

The illustrations in this book were done in
Winsor & Newton oil paints on Strathmore illustration board.
The text type was set in Plantin.
The display type was hand lettered by Tom Seibert.
Color separations by Bright Arts Ltd., Hong Kong
Manufactured by South China Printing Company, Ltd., China
Production supervision by Sandra Grebenar and Pascha Gerlinger
Designed by Ivan Holmes

For Lily
—D. A.

For Tricia Miranda and "Peanut"
—C. O.

"Throw the ball," Mama said.

I threw it into her glove.

"No!" Mama told me. "Make me reach for it. Make me jump."

I threw the ball just over Mama's head. She reached and caught it. I threw the ball again, this time high over her head. She jumped and caught it.

We played a long time. Then we sat on the steps. Mama held my hand. She looked at me and said, "I need a job. While Dad's away, I need to work."

It was wartime. Dad was in the army fighting for our country.

Mama said, "I need your help practicing baseball because I hope to get a job playing in the women's league."

What kind of job is that? I wondered.

Before the war, Dad drove a truck for a milk company. Each morning he brought milk from farms to a plant where it was poured into bottles. That's *a job*, I thought. *Baseball is just a game*.

That night at Sunday dinner Grandpa told me, "I fought in the last war." He showed me his medal.

Grandma said, "You told Amy last night about the war and your medal."

"Well, I did fight and I did win a medal," Grandpa said.

He pointed to an old picture. He'd shown me *that* last night, too.

After dinner we listened to news of the war on the radio. Then we listened to *The Jack Benny Show,* Dad's favorite. I wondered if Dad was listening, too.

The next morning, we went in Grandpa's car to a large baseball stadium. Grandma, Grandpa, and I sat in the stands. Mama went onto the field.

There were a lot of women there. They stood in a line. A man with a bat hit a ball to them. If a woman missed the ball, the man said, "Thank you," and pointed to a gate at the side of the field. That woman didn't make the team.

Finally, it was Mama's turn.

The man hit the ball over Mama's head, just like I threw it to her when we practiced.

Mama reached for the ball and caught it.

Then she went to the back of the line.

Each time it was Mama's turn, she caught the ball.

When the man pitched to the women who were left, Mama swung twice and missed. Then she hit the ball on the ground right back to the man.

It wasn't a good hit.

I was afraid the man would say, "Thank you," and point to the gate.

But he didn't. He told Mama to come back the next day.

Two days later, Mama showed us her uniform. It was a pretty skirt, a shirt with a fancy patch, long socks, a baseball hat, and shoes. *If Mama has a uniform,* I thought, *she must be on the team.*

Mama got the job!

That night we had a party to celebrate Mama's new job. Grandma baked a cake, and I covered it with icing and sprinkles. We kept the radio on as we ate. We listened to news of the war, and I thought about Dad.

At bedtime Mama told me she hoped the war would end soon so Dad would come home. I hoped so, too.

The next week, Grandma and Grandpa took me to one of Mama's games. Her team was in the field. The ball was hit high over Mama's head.

She jumped and reached up. I jumped and reached up, too. Mama caught the ball!

When it was Mama's turn to hit, I stood. The pitcher threw the ball and Mama swung her bat. I swung, too—and hit Grandpa's bag of peanuts.

Peanuts flew everywhere. When I looked back on the field, Mama was standing on second base. She had hit a double. And Grandpa had changed his seat.

"Amy moves around too much," he whispered to Grandma.

"Amy is playing baseball along with her mama," Grandma told him.

When the game was over, I ran to Mama. "We won!" I shouted.

Mama hugged and kissed me. We were so happy.

Grandma, Grandpa, and I went to lots of Mama's games, but only the ones that were nearby. Mama traveled with her team by bus to faraway games. I stayed home and drew pictures. I love to draw.

After each game, people crowded around Mama. They asked her to sign pieces of paper and baseballs.

One day when we got home, I asked Mama to sign a baseball for me.

"You don't need my autograph," she said.

"Oh, yes I do," I told her. "I want it because you're a great baseball player *and* because you're my mother."

That winter, whenever the ground was clear of snow and ice, Mama and I went outside. We wore winter coats. I wore woolen gloves. Mama wore her baseball glove.

Mama gave me a baseball and told me, "Throw the ball. Make me reach for it. Make me jump."

She practiced whenever she could.

"Baseball is my job," she told me. "And I want to be good at it."

It was *my* job to help her.

Then one morning the next fall, Mama put on her uniform. "Come with me," she said. "I have a surprise for you."

"Aren't Grandma and Grandpa coming to the game?"

"No," Mama said. "Just you and me, and we're going to the bus station."

While we walked, I asked Mama, "Are you taking me to a faraway game?"

Mama didn't answer. She just smiled.

When we got to the station, we waited. Then a bus stopped and lots of people got off. Some of them were soldiers.

Then I saw him!

My dad was getting off the bus!

Mama and I ran to him. We hugged and kissed him. Mama touched his cheek and said, "You look so handsome in your uniform."

Dad smiled and said, "And you look so pretty in *yours*."

When we came home, Grandma and Grandpa met us at the front door. Grandpa wore his uniform and medal. And inside was a big WELCOME HOME! sign and a cake.

After we celebrated and ate all the cake, I took Dad's hand and said, "Now I have a surprise for *you*."

"You do?" Dad said.

Mama, Grandma, and Grandpa looked at me and asked, "What surprise do you have?"

I didn't answer. I just told Dad to sit in his favorite chair. I went into my room and brought out my drawings. They were of Mama playing baseball.

"These are great," Dad said.

"Mama is a great baseball player," I said.

Then I turned on the radio. It was Sunday night. I sat on Dad's lap and we all listened and laughed to Dad's favorite program, *The Jack Benny Show.*

The war was over.

My dad was home.

Author's note

During the Second World War, many Major League Baseball players served in the army. In 1943 the All-American Girls' Professional Baseball League was formed for the enjoyment of the people still at home. Many of those people were fighting the enemy, too. They were the factory workers who built ships, planes, and guns for American soldiers. Along with league games, the women's teams played exhibitions at army training camps, visited military hospitals, and sold war bonds. Among the team names were the *Peaches, Blue Sox, Belles, Comets, Chicks, Lassies,* and *Daisies.* The league lasted until 1954 with teams in Illinois, Indiana, Wisconsin, Michigan, and Minnesota.

It was not unusual for families, like the one in this story, to welcome their loved ones home from the war with signs that were hung inside, rather than outside, their homes. They kept the signs out of view of neighbors with loved ones who were either not home yet or killed in battle.